I WON'T GET LOST

MARTHA LAMBERT · illustrated by **KATE DUKE**

≡HARPERCOLLINSPUBLISHERS

Text copyright © 2003 by Martha Lambert Illustrations copyright © 2003 by Kate Duke
Manufactured in China. All rights reserved. www.harperchildrens.com
Library of Congress Cataloging-in-Publication Data
Lambert, Martha Lewis.
I won't get lost / by Martha Lambert ; illustrated by Kate Duke.
     p.   cm.
  Summary: Convinced that he will never get lost, a young dragon doodles instead of learning his
address and telephone number in school.
  ISBN 0-06-028960-0 — ISBN 0-06-028961-9 (lib. bdg.)
  [1. Dragons—Fiction. 2. Lost children—Fiction. 3. Schools—Fiction.] I. Duke, Kate, ill. II. Title.
PZ7.L1696 Iae 2003   2001039289
[Fic]—dc21
Typography by Matt Adamec 1 2 3 4 5 6 7 8 9 10 ❖ First Edition

This book is dedicated to the child beside us and the child within us . . .
may they both always know their heart as their home.

—M.L.

For Sidney

—K.D.

Horatio pouted over his cereal.

"Hurry, Horatio," said Mother. "You'll be late for school."

"I don't want to go," whined Horatio.

Mother and Father looked surprised. "We thought you liked school," they said.

"I do like dragon practice and lunch and recess," said Horatio. "But I don't like the other stuff, and I don't need to know it."

"You need to know more than just how to be a dragon," said Father. "That's why you need to go to school."

Horatio said, "Okay," but he was thinking something else. He was thinking that if he had to go to school, he would only learn the things he liked.

COCOAL PUFFS

After breakfast, everyone helped make the lunches: charcoal sandwiches, Tabasco tea, and Tire Tidbits for dessert. Mother wrapped them, Father packed them, and Horatio held the bags open.

Then they all kissed good-bye. Mother left for the torch factory, Father headed off to the Snack Dragon Bakery, and Horatio started for school.

Horatio had a great morning. Miss Scaley gave a safety lesson on fire breathing, a rioting-and-rampaging test, and a roaring bee, which is like a spelling bee only you get to *roar* the letters.

FIRE TEST RULES
1. Set twigs on fire.
2. Do not set Miss Scaley on fire.

Then it was time for lunch. Horatio crunched his charcoal sandwiches, sipped his Tabasco tea, and shared his Tire Tidbits with his best friend, Sparky. After lunch they all played their favorite game, capture the princess, until Miss Scaley called them inside.

Miss Scaley gave everyone a sheet of paper. "This afternoon you're going to practice writing your name, address, and telephone number," she said. "You'll need to know these things if you ever get lost."

Horatio's hand shot into the air. "I already know my name. I'm Horatio Horndragon! I live in a cave. And I have a telephone with a number on it!"

Miss Scaley smiled. "You'll need to know more than that to get yourself home if you're lost."

"But I won't get lost!" said Horatio. "Not now or ever!"

"No one ever wants to get lost," replied Miss Scaley. "But sometimes it happens. That's why you need to know your address and phone number—to help you find your way home."

Horatio said, "Okay," but he was thinking something else. He was thinking this was not one of the things he liked.

So as everyone else began practicing writing their name, address, and phone number, Horatio doodled dragons. He doodled big dragons and small dragons—all kinds of dragons—until his paper was completely covered.

Finally, Miss Scaley said, "That's all for today, class. I'll see you tomorrow. Keep practicing!"

Horatio waved to his friends and began to walk home.

On the way home, Horatio saw a giant delivery dragon
carrying lots of packages and mail to the neighborhood caves.
"Wow!" he shouted. "I'm going to see where he goes."

Horatio raced over a stream and through the forest after the delivery dragon. When the delivery dragon had finished delivering packages, Horatio stood and watched him leap into the sky and fly back to the post office. "Wow, I wish I could do that!" he said, and started for home.

He hadn't walked very far when something made him stop. The road he was on had suddenly become two roads! "Which one goes to my cave?" he wondered out loud. "Which way do I go?"

Horatio heard a small voice coming from under a big rock.

"Lost, Sonny?"

"Yes," said Horatio, crouching down to see who was talking.

Two beady eyes blinked back at him. "Maybe I can help," said the voice. "I know most of the roads around here. What's your address?"

"I, ummm, I don't know," said Horatio, beginning to cry.

"Well, what's your phone number? I'll call your mother," said the small voice.

"I don't know that either," sobbed Horatio.

The two beady eyes blinked. "Gee, I'm sorry. Wish I could help, but without your address and phone number, there's nothing I can do." Then the two beady eyes disappeared.

Horatio looked at his practice paper. He tried to read his address and telephone number through the doodles, but he couldn't. The sky soon grew dark, and the forest was filled with a herd of scary shadows. Horatio curled up next to a big log and cried, "I wish I were home."

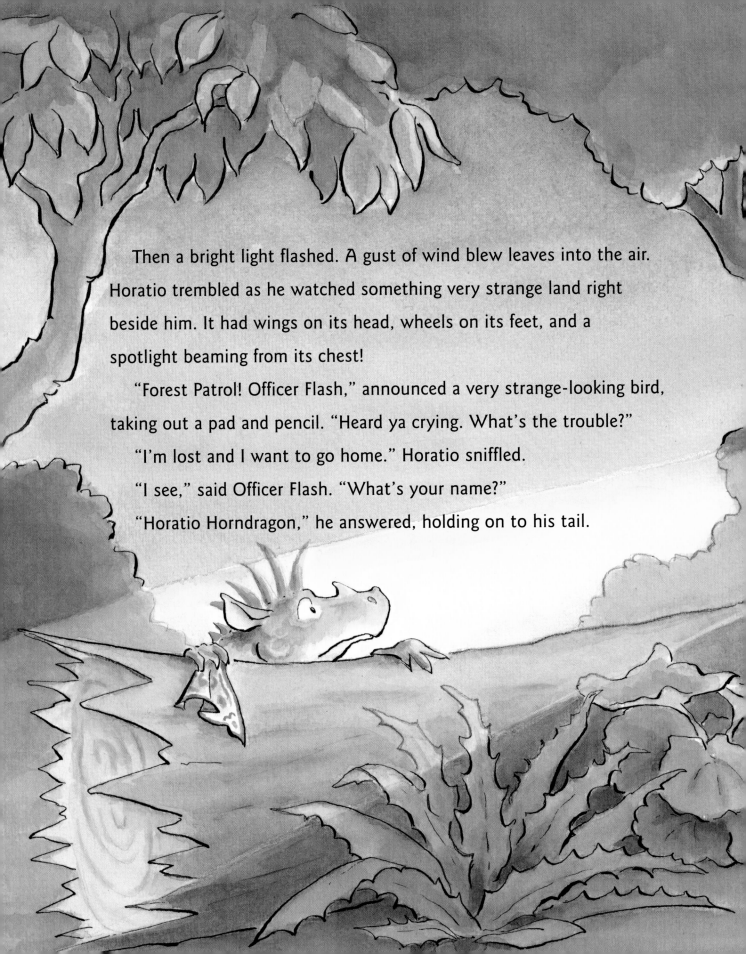

Then a bright light flashed. A gust of wind blew leaves into the air. Horatio trembled as he watched something very strange land right beside him. It had wings on its head, wheels on its feet, and a spotlight beaming from its chest!

"Forest Patrol! Officer Flash," announced a very strange-looking bird, taking out a pad and pencil. "Heard ya crying. What's the trouble?"

"I'm lost and I want to go home." Horatio sniffled.

"I see," said Officer Flash. "What's your name?"

"Horatio Horndragon," he answered, holding on to his tail.

Flash took out his phone: "Flash to base. Come in, base. I'm at the corner of Thunder Boulevard and Ferocious Avenue. I've got a lost dragon here. Green scales. Red spikes. Name's Horatio Horndragon. Do you read me? Over."

"Loud and clear, Flash," said the base operator. "All we need now is an address and a telephone number."

"Understood!" said Flash. "Horatio, we need your address and phone number."

"But I don't *knoooow* them," he wailed.

Flash shook his head. "Base. We have a problem. The little guy only knows his name. Let me know if anyone calls for a young one named Horatio Horndragon."

"Will do. Over and out," answered the operator.

Flash turned off his phone and looked at Horatio. "This might be a long night," he said. "It's too far to walk back to the base. We'll have to stay here until your parents call."

Horatio tried to snuggle as close to Flash as he could.
Every time the radio crackled, Horatio's heart skipped a
beat. "Was that my parents?" he asked.

"Sorry, Horatio, just the regular Forest Patrol stuff. A
flying squirrel crashed into a woodpecker's nest."

Horatio's spikes drooped. He was afraid he might never
get home.

Then suddenly the radio crackled again. Horatio looked up hopefully.

"Come in, base," said Flash. "Any word on the lost dragon?"

"Yes!" said the operator. "A Mr. and Mrs. Horndragon just called. They lost a little dragon named Horatio, green scales, red spikes. They live at Ten Greenscale Lane."

"That's great!" said Flash, checking his map. "We're on our way!"

Horatio jumped for joy.

"Just stay in my spotlight," called Flash. "You'll be home before you know it."

When they arrived home, Horatio's mother and father rushed
over to hug him. "We were so worried!" they cried. "Are you all right?"

"Yes!" shouted Horatio, as his parents hugged him tighter than tight.

Later, when Horatio got ready for bed, he told his parents everything
that had happened. And what he planned to do the next morning
before school.

The next morning when the sun came up, Horatio jumped out of bed and grabbed a piece of paper and pencil. He raced to the mailbox and dashed to the phone.

Then he stood at the breakfast table and said proudly, "Now I know a lot more than how to be a dragon. I know I live at Ten Greenscale Lane and my telephone number is 333-555-7656."

"Hooray for Horatio!" said Mother and Father. "We're very proud of you for learning what you need to know."

Practice Sheet

My name

My address

My phone number

Do you know your address and phone number? If you don't, now is a great time to learn them. And if you do know them, now is a great time to practice. Make a practice paper like Horatio's!